THE Mischief Makers

TONY MCNAMARA

ILLUSTRATIONS- CHRIS BYE

To order additional copies of this book, contact:
Xlibris
UK TFN: 0800 0148620 (Toll Free inside the UK)
UK Local: 02036 956328 (+44 20 3695 6328 from outside the UK)
www.xlibrispublishing.co.uk
Orders@Xlibrispublishing.co.uk

ISBN: 978-1-9845-9507-2 (sc)
ISBN: 978-1-9845-9508-9 (e)

Print information available on the last page.

Rev. date: 10/15/2020

THE CAT, THE FOX AND THE FIRE BRIGADE

I still can't explain how he got up there or why, but the fact was he was there, bold as brass. The white, whiskery tip of his ginger-brown furry nose poking over the edge of my upstairs front bedroom window as he stared down at me - slyly, defiantly, as I stood on the pavement outside the front door, looking up in amazement. That can't possibly be the fox from the field, surely? Our house was at the end of a small cul-de-sac overlooking a large open field, which was used by local football groups and the nearby school for various sporting events and was also home to a family of foxes.

I hastily tried to re-enact my steps since waking up that morning. I had locked the front door as usual before going to bed, closed all the front windows downstairs and checked the same for the back of the house. It was only 8.30 am and I had been alone in the house since my wife had left for work half an hour earlier. And yet there he was! He couldn't have climbed up the side of the house or the gutter on the side edge, could he? Can foxes climb that high? Even if that was physically possible, how had he managed to push himself through the narrow opening offered between the window sill and the open sash window in the upstairs bedroom? None of this made any sense. Even if he had managed that Herculean feat, I am a very light sleeper and would very quickly have been alerted to the noise of a canine intruder in my bedroom. Curiouser and curiouser, to echo what Alice once said when everything around her in her Wonderland was strange, surreal almost – this most peculiar episode still haunts me!

So if he was one of the foxes from the field -"Finn"- as I had named him, he had somehow managed to enter my house via the upstairs bedroom window. Still looking up in disbelief, I noticed that my vulpine victim seemed to have shifted the direction of his gaze and was now looking to the right, still downwards, towards the drainpipe which was fixed to the edge of the house. The gutter ran up from the spout at street level, rising to form a joint with the gutter under the edge of the roof tiles above. I followed his gaze and suddenly noticed a black, plump, furry looking creature, wrapped round the drainpipe about half way between the ground floor and upstairs bedroom window. Oh no! – it was Cornelius the cat from next door! He was often to be seen slinking around the block, slipping sneakily between the parked cars and suitably cat sized gaps beside the bins next to the garage and fencing that marked the field boundary to the far side of my garage, adjacent to the house. I didn't know how to react to the scene unfolding in front of me. Clearly, both Cornelius and Finn needed to be rescued, but who first? And how? My train of thoughts and subsequent action was however soon interrupted by a swift development in events. Finn had jumped out of the window and had pounced down, landing on Cornelius's head, and had managed to fall in such a way that his arms had gripped Cornelius's generous stomach line and allowed his paws to cling on, as his head and body dangled somewhat precariously below Cornelius's chubby frame. What had once seemed to be a singular calamitous event had suddenly become a double -whammy!

I wondered whether to fetch my stepladder, climb up and try to pull them both down and hope they would both then scurry away to their respective nests. A quick calculation of the height of their location on the drainpipe and I soon realised that this was not an option. The ladder would never reach. Looking down, I saw the gravel stones covering my front garden and picking up a handful of the biggest ones, I began to throw them upwards, aiming as best I could at the mass of inter-mingled furriness above. Surely at least one hit would shock them into dislodging their unplanned embrace and shift them both downwards and earthbound?

Alas, it was not to be. Somehow, appearing to defy gravity, sly little Finn was living up to his name and clinging on to Cornelius's generous waistline, with no sign of letting go and Cornelius seemingly oblivious to his unknown attached parasite. In desperation, I began clapping my hands together and making a sort of "shoo – shoo!" noise, looking up and jumping up and down in a frantic attempt to attract their attention. I was beginning to panic now as I seemed to have run out of ideas. Part of me thought I could just leave them to their own devices and hope that sooner or later they would disentangle and scuffle away after landing on the gravel in the front garden at the bottom of the drainpipe. Somehow this didn't feel right. It was then that the answer came to me.

Call the Fire Brigade! They are used to rescuing cats stuck in trees, so surely a cat stuck up a drainpipe attached to a fox would fit the bill? I dashed indoors to ring the Fire Brigade, after a quick last glance at the furry pair. They now seemed to be engaged in a sort of tug-of-war with each others' limbs in an attempt to gain the upper hand and maintain a grip on the drainpipe, accompanied by some horrible screeching and howling noises.

"Hello, yes, this is an emergency call…. which service? – the Fire Brigade please….

The nature of the emergency? …. I hesitated momentarily as I tried to summarise the potentially perilous position outside. "Er, well, it's sort of…a cat and a fox in a bit of a tangle… dangling twenty feet up in the air round my outside drainpipe! I explained that I was worried that they may fall imminently and both could be injured …. or worse! There was a long pause at the other end of the phone as the operator took in what I had just said. After what seemed ages, the voice at the other end of the phone calmly asked for my name and address and advised that the local Fire Brigade had been alerted and would arrive as soon as possible. Feeling somewhat more comfortable in the knowledge that expert help was on its way, I went back outside to the front of the house to review the situation and looked up towards the drainpipe. That sense of comfort and assurance vanished in a second and was replaced by more panic and disbelief.

Cornelius and Finn had somehow managed to disentangle themselves and had climbed up the to the top of the drainpipe and were now perched high up on the tiles on the roof! But they were not just sitting on the tiles, they had managed to find a comfortable ridge tile to perch on and both were now lying on their bellies, side by side, paws outstretched and they were both putting on the most mischievous grin. Suddenly, Finn and Cornelius both leapt to their feet and began dancing together what looked like a foxtrot, across the roof ridge tiles, arm in arm, eyes only for each other, legs stepping together with apparent rehearsed precision. Music suddenly filled the air as a violin magically appeared in Cornelius's outstretched paws and the pair continued to dance together. Impossible though it may sound, they looked as though they were talking to each other and laughing as their furry heads bobbed up and down and the white whiskers on their faces twitched and tweaked.

By now, the Fire Brigade had arrived and the truck had pulled up as close as possible to the front of the house. The eponymous pair had stopped dancing and to my continuing disbelief were now sitting on a striped blanket and were starting to unpack various items from a picnic basket. The Fire Brigade team stared up in astonishment at the unfolding bizarre roof picnic party as onlookers from the street begin to cluster round, gossiping and some taking pictures. The Fire Chief assured me that the situation was nothing unusual and said that he would get a man on a ladder and bring them both down safely. The fire truck's engine gunned into action and soon a long, extendable ladder swung out from the top of the bright red fire truck and extended up towards the roof. A tall, slender looking man, in fireproof overalls and a bright yellow safety helmet began to swiftly ascend the ladder, climbing up towards the rooftop but, as he stepped closer to the top, Cornelius and Finn had now moved up the roof, climbed up the chimney breast and down into the chimney stack. One last cheeky look back and then they suddenly disappeared down the chimney!

The Fire Officer climbed up on to the chimney. He looked down the chimney opening and shone his torch down in to the darkness below. He looked puzzled and shouted back down – "No sign of them!" The Fire chief scratched his head awkwardly. "They must be stuck in the chimney." he sighed. "But it's blocked at the bottom of the fireplace in the lounge!" I exclaimed, realising that where the former open fireplace would have been at the chimney base, there was now an artificial gas fire which sealed off the chimney.

I thought that I would never see my furry friends again and was just about to give up hope of any rescue attempt when I had a moment of inspiration and remembered that I had kept a copy of the architect's plans of the house with the layout and measurements of the building. I had carefully filed the plans away for a "just in case" situation- such as this. The plans, somewhat faded with time and with a slightly damp, dank, smell, still showed all the technical specifications of the original Victorian building construction, including the land plot boundaries, wall construction details, foundations and drainage and sewerage outlets, but, more importantly, diagrams of the chimney and ventilation shafts!

Closer inspection of the chimney duct revealed that the there was a small shaft at the base of the chimney top, like a tunnel, which extended across the rear side of the roof, exiting via a ventilation plate. When the house was first built, this was located at the outward facing end of the ceiling of the rear upstairs bedroom. Over the years, however, that plate had been sealed up and plastered over and there was no other visible exit on the plans which would have allowed the fleeing friends to escape. So, were they trapped? The tunnel was far too narrow for a Fire Brigade person to crawl through. The rope attached to the hydraulic crane on the fire-truck would not be able to extend down the tunnel and the powerful water hoses would not have enough force to extend to reach the small duct and flush them out. It seemed as though there was nothing else the Fire Brigade could do. The Fire Chief said sorry and suggested that perhaps the Local Authority Pest Control Team may be able to help. The fire truck drove away.

Pest Control? I pictured the two poor little creatures stuck in the sooty darkness of the chimney and I knew that this was not an option – there must be something I could do! The crowd of onlookers had now dispersed to go about their business and there was only me left standing, alone on the pavement. I walked through the house to check out the view from the back garden, looking up at the rear upstairs bedroom. As I looked up at the back of the house, I smiled and my heart fluttered. Could there have been another shaft coming off the main tunnel of the chimney duct, which turned back towards the loft space under the front sloping part of the roof? This section of the loft space under the roof was closed off from the converted loft room which had been built on to the house long after the original Victorian building was erected, so any other ventilation ducts or shafts added to the building would not have been included in the original building plans. This loft space was still accessible from inside the house via a small wooden hatch from the loft bedroom. I used the front part of the loft space for storage but most of the area had only the original wooden joists for a floor so it wasn't possible to walk on – well not for fully grown man – but a nimble little fox or cat would be able to tiptoe quite easily across the joists and this dark enclosed space would also be the perfect hiding place! That is, assuming that they had managed to successfully navigate their way along the ventilation shaft in complete darkness, had then found the other shaft and somehow emerged in the loft!

I weighed up possible alternative scenarios. Was the shaft a worm hole and Cornelius and Finn had been whisked away to some parallel world or invisible dimension and would never be seen again? Highly unlikely. Could they have dug another tunnel out of the chimney or, forced their way out from the chimney base by smashing through the gas fire, emerging in the lounge and then scurrying away into the garden by the back door? The only other alternative, that they were stuck midway in the tunnel and would almost certainly die of starvation and exhaustion, was almost too unbearable to contemplate. So, as a certain Mr. Holmes once said, when you have eliminated the impossible, whatever is left, however improbable, must be the case.

I unlocked the padlock securing the wooden loft hatch, torch in the other hand, and bent down on all fours as I pushed myself through the hatch in to the sloping loft space ahead. The brightness of the light beam from the torch pierced the inky blackness around me and lit up the wooden floor joists and roof rafters one at a time as the torch panned across from left to right. Out of the pitch dark at the far right of the loft, something grabbed my attention. What at first sight looked like two very small pairs of fairy lights, close together, were twinkling at me from out of the gloom…. and there they were! As the torch lit up the far corner, my feline fugitive and crafty canine cousin were curled up together, at the very edge of the sloping roof where the wooden roof joists met the front of the house. Looking surprisingly relaxed, but with fur a bit blackened with sooty remnants and dust from the chimney! Well, I was just glad to see that they were safe and disregarded any further thoughts about what I should do next. I suppose they weren't doing any harm up here and I rarely had any need to access this place and, if they had tunnelled their way up here, I'm sure they would find their way back out. Just in case, I didn't padlock the loft hatch and left it slightly ajar.

Before I ducked down to ease myself back through the hatch into the loft bedroom, I turned back for one last look at my newly found squatters and I shone the torch across their faces briefly – what was that round the chain on Finn's furry neckline? The small, bronze, metallic object shone briefly as it reflected the torchlight. Surely that's not my front door key? If I didn't know better, I almost thought I saw Finn wink at me!

CORNELIUS AND FINN GO FOR A SPIN

It was Halloween – my favourite night of the year and I was really looking forward to it. I had been rummaging around in my fancy dress box in the garage, sorting through the scary masks, deciding what to wear to the party later. I used to have at least six different costumes and masks to wear for Halloween. Somewhere I had heard that six was thought by some people to be a lucky number. It was the best score you could achieve from rolling a dice so that could bring you luck in some games. In mathematics it was known as a perfect number and in China, the number six was said to bring good fortune. It also happened to be my house number. I was shortly to find however that this number was not going to bring me either good luck of fortune – in fact, quite the opposite! That number would manifest itself as a series of seemingly random household items which would soon be mysteriously connected and weave a tale of mischief and magic!

It all started with the missing car keys. Every day, after parking the car on the drive, I would routinely place the car keys in the wooden tray at the front of the drawer in the sideboard in the living room, among various other keys; the tape measure and the odd nut, bolt and loose battery. I had tipped out and sorted through the entire tray contents, managing to find the small screwdriver which I thought I had lost, but the car keys just weren't there! Scratching my head and thinking I must have put them somewhere else, I thoroughly searched the other drawer and the bottom cupboard but, there was still no sign of the keys. They were definitely there last night and nothing else seemed to be missing so, I ruled out the possibility of a burglary and anyway, there had been no sign of any break- in. I needed a distraction.

Feeling peckish, I opened the fridge door and was looking forward to snacking on that delicious joint of cider smoked ham. But where was it? I'm sure it was at the front of the bottom shelf yesterday evening. Searching the fridge contents and pulling various jars and packets out on to the table, I became increasingly frustrated as the long-anticipated meat feast continued to evade me. Despite my best efforts, the ham joint was nowhere to be seen. This was too much to be a coincidence – losing car keys was bad enough but a vanishing ham joint? Who had been raiding my fridge and also stealing my car keys? Two unrelated, missing things. There was only one set of car keys which I had definitely placed in the key drawer and last night I had cut off some of the ham joint for dinner and then put it back in the fridge.

Before checking that the car was on the drive, I remembered that I needed to get the monster masks and hat from the fancy-dress box in the garage ready for the Halloween party later.

I pulled the fancy dress box down from the storage shelf in the garage. The Japanese Samurai spirit face mask and zombie face mask, my favourite fancy dress props, weren't in the box. Neither was my white Fedora gangster hat. It may sound odd, but when people asked me who or what I was supposed to be when I went to a fancy dress party wearing the Fedora and the Japanese face mask, I would say that I was Al Capone's long-lost Japanese brother! But the Japanese mask wasn't just any ordinary plastic mould of typical Halloween scary monsters and ghouls. It was a copy of a legendary Japanese demon – Banioba. According to the legend, the mask face possessed the ability when worn, to transport the wearer of the mask and a person next to them, to any place they wished. I felt a sense of loss and disappointment at the disappearance of my favourite masks and hat. So this was now the third unexplained disappearance.

But then I noticed that other items from the garage were also missing from their usual place. I kept a pile of old house bricks in one corner of the garage. These had earned their long-term spot in the limited space in the garage by a useful, occasional wedging or propping up in various ad-hoc household jobs. I noticed that the pile of bricks had been dislodged and two were missing from the top of the pile. Next to the bricks was stored a loop of white rope and this too, was missing. The storage cupboard doors were open and some of the patio chair cushions had spilled out on to the concrete garage floor. I tidied them away but then counting them back in the cupboard, realised that three of the six cushions were unaccounted for.

Keys, meat, fancy dress props, bricks, rope and seat cushions – six seemingly random objects, all vanished without a trace and with no clue as to how or why they had disappeared. Reflecting on earlier incidents, I thought that if the car keys had gone missing, I had better check that the car was still parked on the front drive.

My heart missed a beat as I stepped out of the front door and looked towards the drive where I had parked the car last night. There was a big, empty space on the gravel where the car had been. It was as if it had never been there or had been whisked away by persons or other unidentified entities unknown. I couldn't believe my eyes. Pinching my cheek firmly to check that this wasn't a scary dream, I tried to work out what to do next.

Retracing my steps, I noticed a tell-tale piece of crucial evidence which led me to believe who the culprits responsible for the six- fold theft were. A more detailed scrutiny of the fridge contents revealed a small imprint in the butter tray. After discounting the random shapes created across the soft creamy surface of the butter from various swipes and jabs with the butter knife; a distinctive, claw like mark was there in the butter. There was no doubt in my mind - it was unmistakably a fox paw print! My head was spinning – I hadn't seen Cornelius the cat and Finn the fox, my two furry fugitive domestic squatters, for a few days. I last saw them huddling together in their secluded loft hatch nest, looking very peaceful and content.

I had to check to ensure that they were still there and entered the loft room. The loft hatch door was open. I hadn't locked it so it would be easy to push open from the inside. Peering in through the hatch into the darkness of the sloping loft rafter space, my torch scanned across from left to right and the torch beam found nothing. My head was spinning at the thought of my missing car and furry colleagues. I had to phone the police to report a stolen vehicle – but what about the missing items from the garage? Should I report these as missing or stolen? There was no evidence of a break-in, so the Police wouldn't be able to do anything. I needed some thinking time so I made a cup of tea and sat down and turned on the TV.

I nearly lost my grip on my mug as I saw the latest news bulletin and listened in disbelief to what the newscaster was reporting. The TV screen showed CCTV footage of a vehicle seen speeding down the highway, swerving erratically and weaving between the lanes, missing other vehicles by a whisker and showing no sign of slowing down. From the slightly blurred CCTV camera footage, I could just about see the car's vehicle registration number – It was mine! – However, because of the height of the CCTV camera, the newscaster commented, the driver's identity was uncertain. Subsequent footage from close ups revealed that the driver seemed to have a very hairy profile outline and was wearing a red mask and a white wide brimmed hat. The passenger seat was occupied by a smaller hairy faced individual, wearing a white mask. Zooming in further, the camera revealed what appeared to be a ham bone with gnaw marks on the back seat. I shut my eyes and waited for a few seconds, thinking that I had just had a very vivid daydream and then opened my eyes – only to see further cctv footage of my car. The driver's face, obscured by the red mask, was barely visible above the dashboard through the front windscreen. Latest reports said that the vehicle was last seen heading towards Epping Forest but that they had been unable to track the exact whereabouts of the runaway car and there was no clear lead as to the identity of who had taken the car and driven it away.

My mind raced as I tried to piece together the seemingly impossible events that had led up to this TV footage of my runaway car and the two most unlikely car thieves. Before going to bed and deciding on next steps, I made one last check of my furry friends' nest in the roof section of the loft room, via the loft hatch. They weren't there.

After a restless night, I awoke with a start to a loud knocking on the front door and dashed downstairs in my pyjamas to see who was there. Two police officers were standing on the front step of the porch, holding a clipboard and looking very concerned. They confirmed my name and address and vehicle details and then advised me that my car had been reported as abandoned in a picnic parking site in Epping Forest. After paying the vehicle tow away and return fee, the Police handed over the car keys and pointed out that the vehicle was parked on the road outside my house. They were pleased to let me know there had been no damage to the vehicle but that there were a few additional items which had been noted in the inventory list of vehicle contents handed over when I had signed for the car keys. The list read - front seats - two house bricks, with a length of white rope attached and on the back seats, two masks and a ham bone. I was puzzled as to why they had gone to the trouble of listing those extra items, but there was no mention of who the mysterious masked driver and passenger may have been. I thanked the Police officers for returning my car safely and hurried towards the vehicle to inspect the contents.

I approached the car slowly and looked down through the windows to see what was inside. There was no sign of Cornelius and Finn. Where were they? Then I noticed the two decorated masks on the back seat, one red and one white. I picked up the red mask – it was unmistakeably my Japanese Samurai mask! I gazed at the slightly scary, wide, red mouth. The wide lips were framed in a bright halo of shiny white paint, edged in a metallic bronze colour. An almost demonic grin seemed to spread right across the surface of the mask's shiny plastic face. The eyebrows above, and long, curly eyelashes beneath the empty spaces where the wearer's eyes would peep out, radiated a slimy green brilliance. The longer I stared at the mask, the more I found it difficult to look away. It was almost as if the mask was hypnotising me! I was distracted by the loud slamming of a car door parked on the opposite side of the road which snapped me out of my demonic reverie and a seemingly impossible idea suddenly came into my mind. What if the legend of the mask's power to transport the wearer, and a companion, if they were next to each other, to wherever they wished, were true? But where would Finn and Cornelius go? Did they wish themselves deep in to Epping Forest, near where the car was found, or somewhere else? Did they know any other places, apart the field next to my house and their nest up in the loft? I decided to check the car again to make sure it was still roadworthy and everything was working as normal.

I then spotted the two bricks on the floor on the driver's side, resting on the brake and accelerator foot pedals. The car was an automatic, so there was no clutch pedal. Coils of white rope were wrapped round each brick, extending to about three feet in length. On the driver's seat were three pale cream striped cushions, piled up one on top of the other. So that's how they did it! I realised.

Starting up the engine, I pushed the gear lever into the drive position which engaged the drive into forward motion. I lifted up one of the lengths of rope with the brick attached and let it down slowly until the brick gently made contact with the accelerator pedal. Leaving it there but keeping hold of the end of the rope, I gradually loosened my grip on the rope and gravity did the rest- the weight of the brick pressed down on the pedal and the engine began to rev faster and the car gently eased forward. I carried out the same series of manoeuvres with the rope and the other brick on the brake pedal and the car eased to a halt.

A quick glance down at the pile of cushions and back up to the controls and driver's view out of the front windscreen and it was clear that the height of the cushions on top of the driver's seat would provide just enough lift to allow a small furry creature to have a clear view of the road ahead through the windscreen. So, the mystery of the vanishing vehicle and spin at speed down the dual carriageway was solved. But where were Cornelius and Finn? Were they still roaming around in the wilds of Epping Forest or had they taken up residence in someone else's loft or roof? A feeling of sadness suddenly came over me as I feared that I may never know what had happened to my furry friends and I went back in to the house and sat down, exhausted.

Drifting off into a pleasant light sleepy, dream-like state, visions of Finn and Cornelius seemed to materialise in front of my eyes, as if from nowhere, and then smiling, their shadowy forms disappeared in an instant through the ceiling above my head. Springing back to life and looking up, I ran up the stairs to the loft room and, torch in hand, crawled up to and opened the loft hatch and shone my torch towards the far side of the chamber where the sloping roof timbers met the wooden floor joists.

There they were, curled up asleep in their blanket! I shone my torch over the furry pair and noticed small crumbs of pastry crust around Finn's furry face whiskers. I had obviously missed the pork pie in my earlier search of the fridge! A small piece of white rope was also curled snake-like on the carpet next to Cornelius. Stunned by the bright torch light, they both suddenly looked up at me, with faces seemingly innocent of any possible mischief. It was then that I thought, if only they could talk, the expression on their faces would surely have said "We were only having a bit of fun!"

MERLIN THE MAGIC GARDEN GNOME

The back garden was finally finished! I looked out at the newly landscaped beds, paving stones and patio area and thought that although it looked so much better than before, there was still something missing. There was the green, metal bird bath stand, to the left of the patio at the bottom of the garden, and on the opposite side, under the shade of the curling, climbing honeysuckle, was a small pond with a fountain in the middle.

What else would give the garden a lift and sit well with the existing decorative items? Browsing around the local garden centre, I passed the water fountains and bird feeders and, turning the corner, I suddenly saw just the thing! Staring back at me was a green faced, bearded, gnome ornament, with a long pointed red hat. He had a bright pink, bulbous nose and white flowing locks of hair and was holding what looked like a magic staff with a bright red lantern at the end.

Fascinated by this creature of many fables and myths, which stood over six feet tall and was almost hidden among the surrounding shrubs and plants, I approached for a closer look. I had never been a particular fan of garden gnomes. Some people made them a feature of their garden with whole families of gnomes clustered together, holding fishing rods around a pond, sitting on brightly coloured mushrooms, or carrying axes and other garden tools. But something about this one fascinated me. Perhaps it reminded me of a famous wizard that I had seen or heard of in all those childhood fairy stories and adventures.

Either side of the gnome's bright pink nose were dark, diamond shaped eyes, set deeply in their sockets. Above his eyes were the bushiest, whitest eyebrows imaginable. I was struck by the incredible detail in the sculpting of the facial features and the way the white beard seemed to flow like a waterfall from the gnome's mouth down to below his neck. This attention to detail I had not seen before on any other garden gnome furniture.

A long, purple cloak was draped across the gnome's shoulders, flowing down over his arms and was secured by a gold coloured clasp beneath his neck. In his beard and around his belt were hung several gold rings and on closer inspection, I noticed some sort of engraving on the gold clasp on the cloak around his neck. It was a name! Merlin. That's unusual, I thought, I didn't know gnomes were individually named. Perhaps this was a special edition gnome which someone had decided to elaborately paint as a one-off? I decided that Merlin deserved a spot in my back garden and I would position him, pride of place, in the flower bed in the middle of the patio! He would be the central feature of the bottom patio area, nestling between the climbing clematis and roses, in front of the trellis. His purple cloak and the splash of gold on the clasp and gold rings in his beard and belt would perfectly complement the pink and red hues of the clematis and roses which curled and climbed up the wooden trellis in front of the side fence bordering the field.

Having positioned Merlin securely in place in the bed as I had pictured, I sat at the patio table, sipping a cup of tea, feeling a sense of completeness looking across at the bed space he now occupied which had previously seemed somehow empty. The next day I decided to water the plants as it hadn't rained for a while. I filled the watering can to the brim and began sprinkling the can's nutritious contents over the various terracotta pots which were scattered around the garden. I reached the bottom patio bed and smiled at the sight of Merlin's face as water droplets bounced off his hat and over his flowing cloak. The stream of water pouring from the green metal watering can soaked the leaves and blossoms of the clematis and roses. But wait a minute, I thought. I don't remember these climbers being this high yesterday? The clematis and rose seemed to be almost twice as high and had sprouted several more flowers and new buds. On the other side of the garden, the sunflowers and the rhododendrons also seemed to have shot up in size and the pond and fountain had inexplicably moved from the right side of the patio and were now situated snuggly alongside Merlin in the bed on the left side of the patio!

In a state of shock, I put the watering can down, pulled up a chair at the side of the patio table and collapsed down on to the cushioned seat.

I rubbed my eyes and then looked across the garden again from left to right and stared in disbelief at the apparent sudden growth of the plants and shrubs and the relocation of the pond. My wife may have moved the pond without my knowledge but, green fingered in the garden as she may be, she couldn't make plants grow to twice their height overnight! I decided to shrug it off and not worry about it anymore, teasing myself into thinking that it was "the fairies who live at the bottom of the garden" who were to blame, as my mother used to say to me when she used to make up stories when I was a young lad.

Later that evening, with a full moon shining brightly in a cloudless night sky, I stood on the paving outside the Kitchen and looked skyward and scanned across the horizon for the faint sparkle of distant stars. Glancing back down to the bottom of the garden, in the darkness, my eyes caught sight of two small specks of what looked like fairy lights, resembling the dim white reflected light from the solar garden lights. But there was another, red light, slightly higher but very near the two white lights. I don't remember having bought any more solar garden lights, I pondered, as I stared at the dim glow from the bottom of the garden. Then, walking down the garden path towards the source of the lights, I saw that they were coming from Merlin!

I crouched down close to the trellis where Merlin was ensconced in the bed among the plants and climbers in front of the trellis. There it was in plain sight, seeming to defy any logical explanation – a twinkle of white light shone out from the centre of each of Merlin's diamond shaped eye sockets and, looking up and following the length of his raised left arm, a pale red light radiated from the lantern at the end of his staff. I bent down and quickly checked behind and around the glowing gnome to feel for any wires, batteries, or other electrical appliances which may have explained the source of the light emanating from this piece of supposedly inanimate painted terracotta. But my search was in vain and on closer inspection of the eyes and lantern, I was mystified as to how or why my little Merlin gnome was manifesting what I could only describe as a magical light display. I wondered whether the full moon's light over the garden was playing tricks on my vision and decided to return indoors to the comfort of my lounge.

The next morning, my wife woke me saying that the back garden needed some urgent attention. She didn't have time to fully explain what exactly was needed as she was in a rush to leave for work but, I did recall something about the amount of weeds and long, trailing tentacles of ivy, which seemed to have grown over the bed borders and were straggling across and over the path paving stones down to the patio.

I stepped out from the kitchen door on to the small paved area overlooking the lawn and path and the border bed. But there was barely any path to be seen. It was as if all the plants and shrubs in the border bed had produced several years' growth overnight and in particular, the long tentacle-like spread of the ivy had extended its grasp right along the path. The flowers and shrubs had grown so large that they had completely smothered Merlin and only the top of his pointed hat was visible.

I headed for the garage to find an axe, planning to cut back all this unwanted garden growth as quickly as possible. Returning to the back garden after only minutes, the jungle like growth had increased rapidly and the garden was now unrecognisable. The previously neatly trimmed lawn grass was now a jungle of twisting vines and creeping tendrils which soared thirty feet or more in the air. I couldn't see the bottom of the garden. I had to reach the patio area. I was now sure that somehow Merlin had something to do with all the recent strange happenings in the garden. I picked up the axe and started to hack my way into and through the dense jungle.

The axe soon began to clear a path through the thick, dark foliage. Ducking between trailing creepers and climbing over sprawling tree roots, I felt as though I had reached the tropics and was immersed deep in the Amazonian forest. My eyes were met with exotic, tropical like species of rainbow coloured, flowers with huge drooping petals and shiny green translucent shrubs and plants. I heard strange high - pitched bird song and also spotted a number of large, long legged, green glowing spiders clinging to tree trunks and hairy insect-like creatures which I had never seen before, scuttling across the foliage.

After what seemed hours of intense hacking and chopping my way through the jungle-like foliage, I found myself emerging from the darkness into what looked like a clearing ahead. It was as if a giant had trodden a random path through the tropical undergrowth and had cleared the way ahead. The brightness of the sun's rays pierced the inky darkness of the surrounding jungle and momentarily my eyes blinked as I adjusted to the sudden change in the unfolding environment in front of me. Ahead of me, I gazed in disbelief at what looked like a scene from a fairy tale.

There was a gap in the dense foliage ahead which revealed a clearing, with a grassy meadow, covered with exotic, tropical-like flowers, some so intensely reflecting the sun's rays that their petals seemed almost luminous. And what were those strange, rainbow coloured fish jumping above the lake's shimmering surface, pausing momentarily in mid-air as if frozen in time, before swooping back down and disappearing under the silvery surface of this enchanted lake. The silvery, shiny lake was fed by a huge waterfall, the mouth of which spouted from a gap in a rock formation above the back of the lake, which towered high into the clearing and disappeared in the mist beyond.

I had never seen such a spectacle.

Through the watery mist pouring from the rockface, I caught a glimpse of what looked like Merlin, perched on a rock behind the lip of where the waterfall gushed down to the lake below.

I noticed that the closer that I got to the waterfall, Merlin seemed to somehow fade behind the silvery cascade of the torrent before me. A quick, enigmatic smile and a wave and suddenly Merlin was gone.

I clambered up the slimy rocks around the edge of the waterfall and reached the cavernous dome underneath the edge of the rock face where the waterfall plunged down into the lake below. I carefully looked around the surrounding rocks and cavern area but Merlin was nowhere to be seen. My eyes suddenly caught sight of a small, rolled up piece of what looked like a parchment or scroll, with a green coloured wax seal across it, resting on top of one of the larger boulders near the edge of the waterfall.

Well, things couldn't really get any stranger, could they? Merlin, who I thought I had glimpsed in the waterfall, had suddenly disappeared into the mist and I was beginning to find it difficult to trust my senses in this bizarre jungle landscape, as the borderline between fantasy and reality seemed increasingly blurred. I decided to open the parchment and see what message or information may be inside. I unrolled it carefully and saw that it contained a strange verse, written in a glowing green coloured ink. It was signed at the bottom – Merlin, the magic gnome. I took a deep breath and read the full verse......

"THROUGH MY JUNGLE YOU HAVE TREKKED,
HOPING TO FIND ME, I EXPECT!
BUT A JUST A GLIMPSE AND I WAS GONE,
AWAY IN THE MIST TO BACK AND BEYOND,
LEAVING YOU ALONE BY THE POND;
BUT AS MY ONLY HONOURED GUEST,
I LEAVE YOU WITH NOT A CHALLENGING QUEST,
IF YOUR GARDEN YOU WISH TO RESTORE,
TO ME BRING THREE THINGS WHICH I TRULY ADORE;
THREE GOLDEN RINGS, TWENTY-TWO CARAT, UPON YOUR OATH!
OR ELSE........... FOREVER YOU WILL LIVE IN THE UNDER-GROWTH!

I didn't know what the scroll may contain, but I certainly hadn't bargained on its being a quest with a rather horrible ending if I failed to complete the task! I sat down on the slimy, wet rock on which the parchment had been so carefully placed, feeling suddenly very weary and not knowing what to do next.

Three gold rings I could probably obtain without too much difficulty, if I managed to follow the same path back through the jungle to my house. But I hadn't left any sort of markers on my way to the waterfall – what if I never found the way out? And even if I escaped, I wasn't even sure that I could find the pure twenty - two carat gold rings Merlin wanted. Now all those rings I had seen on his belt and beard when I first brought him in to the garden made sense. He clearly loved collecting rings! My heart almost missed a beat at the next thought that popped in to my mind. What if he collects people, as well! Had he done this before to other people who had bought Merlin in to their gardens, leaving them stranded in jungles or who knows what other horrible places if they had failed to fulfil his quests?

The prospect of being left alone in a hostile jungle spurred me in to action and I jumped off the rock and clambered down the rocks at the side of the waterfall as quickly and carefully as I could. Looking back across the lake, I caught sight of a gap in the long, twisting vines and tree trunks and headed towards it hoping that this was where I had originally emerged from the darkness and gloom of my jungle prison. I still had my axe and managed to hack through some stubborn overhanging branches and creeping vine tendrils, opening up what looked like a clearer path through the dense foliage. I looked up to the jungle canopy soaring high above my head for any traces of sunlight which may help guide me back home. The tree branches and leaves were so thick and dense nearer the jungle canopy that not even a single beam of sunlight could penetrate the inky gloom. But then as my eyes adjusted to the darkness, I saw the faint green glow of the giant tree spiders which I had seen on my way here. At first, they seemed to be located randomly, perched near the bottom of the tree trunks and sprawling roots of some of the larger trees. But then I noticed that the trees that most of the spiders were clinging to formed a sort of channel through the dense jungle ahead of me. The jungle's own natural navigation beacons! I eagerly started to follow the luminous trail of my glowing guides.

I didn't have time to visit shops or jewellery stores to buy the three gold rings so once I was back home, I began to search frantically through my wife's jewellery box in the hope of finding at least one or two gold rings. After a long rummage, I found two gold rings in the box, not knowing their carat purity but just hoping that they would meet Merlin's criteria. But Merlin had asked for three gold rings! Where would I find a third ring without going on a long shopping spree? I looked down at my hands holding the two rings and suddenly saw the answer right in front of me – I had forgotten that I was wearing a gold ring!

I wrapped the three rings securely and headed back through the jungle, this time to be sure of a certain route back, I made marks on the trees along the way with my axe, just in case the mysterious luminous spiders disappeared! I arrived at the waterfall and climbing up the rocks to the cavern behind, I found a passage at the back which led out into a wider, open, grassy, meadow like space which extended what seemed like acres in front of me, disappearing into the far horizon. It was as if the strange jungle had never existed. The sun was shining and I made quick progress as I walked briskly through the grassy meadow ahead. After a while, I could see some familiar looking shrubs and plants – it looked like the bottom of my garden! It was a joy to see the butterflies dancing across the grass and to hear familiar birdsong. Such a sweet sound after the strangely alien sounding squawks and squeals of the jungle which I had become accustomed to during my long trek through the dark foliage.

I then spotted Merlin, still standing in the same place in the bed in which I had originally put him. There he was, looking as innocent as the day I first placed him in the garden bed but the expression on his face seemed to have changed and was now beaming with the most mischievous grin! I approached with caution, the three rings in my hand, expecting him to say something or cast a spell on me but he remained as still as stone. There was nowhere I could see to attach the three rings on to Merlin's belt or cloak so I placed them delicately over his outstretched left arm, on to the tip of the lantern on the end of his magic staff, which still glimmered with a faint red light even in daylight. I stood back and waited for something to happen, anticipating some sign in recognition that I had fulfilled Merlin's conquest. I held my breath and just hoped that the jungle would disappear and that the whole of my lovely back garden would come back.

Nothing happened. I waited longer and then in desperation, shouted at the now seemingly inert terracotta figure in front of me to kindly go and leave me and my garden in peace! I tried to dig around Merlin's base and loosen up the surrounding soil and started pulling upwards on his arms with all my strength but he just wouldn't budge. I wiggled him from side to side and back and forth like trying to move a stubborn, well established root bowl on a small tree or shrub, but still no luck! Then I put my hand down under the left side of the gnome and to my horror, I felt a large twisty root which came out of the soil and up into Merlin's terracotta base. Gripping the other side, I reached down into the soil with my other hand and made contact with another chunky root which also ran up from the ground towards the base of the naughty gnome. What on earth was going on! I realised that I couldn't do any more and headed back through the meadow and along the path I had laid in my garden jungle, towards the sanctuary of my house.

I needed more information. Opening Google search for Gnomes and Merlin on my laptop, I waited anxiously as the search engine provided a number of different references to King Arthur's famous wizard Merlin and various anecdotes relating to gnomic mythology, local gnome collectors' groups and suppliers of gnomes and gnome accessories.

So, where did gnomes come from and what was their purpose? I thought that I may somehow become enlightened and find the answer to return my garden to normality and be rid of that evil gnome with seemingly magical powers.

I remembered the stories of Merlin the wizard, who it was alleged was the most powerful sorcerer that had ever been, from the legends of King Arthur and the Knights of the Round Table at Camelot. According to some legends, Merlin possessed the power to be able to change his appearance and physical body into any shape, object, or person.

Gnomes were said to bring good luck to your garden. Not in my case, it would seem indeed, quite the contrary! Other stories of gnomic activity associated their origins with the earth and minerals, even reporting that they would sometimes find gold in your garden! As if he didn't have enough gold already! But nothing I saw made any sense or seemed to shed any light on the origins of my seemingly magical gnome.

In desperation, I returned to the garden centre where I bought my luckless garden ornament in the hope of obtaining some advice as to how to dispose of it or at least uproot it. I found myself struggling to explain to the helpful garden centre staff exactly what the problem was. The manager, a small, bald man with a wrinkled face and white beard, soon approached and asked if he could be of assistance.

"Ah, I see!" he said with a knowing smile. "So, Merlin has been up to his tricks again, has he?" How did he know what Merlin was capable of? He winked and said "No need to worry, I've got just the thing you need, follow me please."

"This will do the trick," he remarked casually, producing a small, round, green tin with a silver lid. "Just make sure that you follow the instructions on the side of the tin carefully. You're lucky, that's the last tin we have." "It's the only thing that works in your situation," he continued. My situation? That seemed to be somewhat of an understatement given the nightmarish train of events which had unfolded since having purchased that pointy hatted, white bearded beast called Merlin!

I paid and thanked the Manager for his help. On the way back home, his other words of advice, repeating what was written on the side of the tin, echoed in my mind. "Rid -o -Gnome" - the only known, tried and tested product for removing unwanted terra-cotta decorative garden gnomes. The ingredients? Top secret! Simply sprinkle a small quantity over the surface of the offending piece and whisper quietly, three times, "go away, gnome, please leave my home!" Leave for twenty-four hours and then return to check for any messages. It all sounded like gobbledegook, especially the last bit – messages? Ah well, I had nothing to lose except my sanity, so decided to give it a go and followed my path back through the jungle of my former prized lawn, to the patio space where Merlin was situated at the bottom of what looked like the remnants of my original back garden. He was still there; although part of me somehow expected him to have just vanished into thin air. Opening the tin lid carefully, I followed the instructions as directed and returned home, following the now familiar jungle path.

The next day, after a restless night's sleep, I was determined to check whether the rid-o-gnome remedy had worked and peered anxiously out of the kitchen window on to the back garden. I did a double blink. Were my eyes playing tricks on me now? The lawn was back to its neatly trimmed former glory, there was no sign of any jungle, trailing vines or other exotic flora or fauna and, miraculously, no sign of Merlin! I looked down at the soil on the spot in the bed where he had previously been standing. A small circle of green dust was all that remained. On closer examination, there was what seemed to be some sort of message written in the dust – it read "Bye – for now – I hope you enjoyed the show!" Digging down further into the dust and earth beneath, my fingers made contact with a hard, smooth object. Reaching further down, my hand found the edge of one side of what felt like a heavy, thin, brick-like block and with a small tug, the loose soil around it soon fell away allowing me to pull the mysterious object to the surface. Brushing away the last remnants of soil and dust, I found myself holding a very heavy, dark yellow, brick-like object. It was approximately a foot long, four inches wide and three inches in depth. Turning towards the light to obtain a better view of the mysterious brick, it suddenly gleamed and sparkled as it reflected the sun shining down on its smooth, even surface. I felt my jaw drop in sheer disbelief as I realised what I was holding – a bar of solid gold! I smiled at my newly found treasure and said aloud "And there was me thinking that it was only Leprechauns that brought you gold!"

.........A MESSAGE FROM MERLIN TO EVERYONE READING HIS STORY!

I HOPE YOU ENJOYED MY MAGICAL TALE,
WE TRAVELLED THROUGH JUNGLE AND OVER THE VALE;
I GAVE AWAY GOLD! WHAT A STORY TO BE TOLD!
MISCHIEF AND MAGIC, BUT NOT REALLY TRAGIC.
CORNELIUS AND FINN- THEY WEREN'T FEATURED IN;
BUT LOOK CLOSER AT THE PAGES
AND YOU MAY SPY THEIR FURRY FACES!

Printed in the United States
By Bookmasters